Tool School

Tool

For George Hallowell — JH

ISBN 978-1-338-23326-1
10 9 8 7 6 5 4 3 2 1   17 18 19 20 21
Printed in the U.S.A.   40

First printing 2017
Book design by Charles Kreloff and Steve Ponzo

120 VOLTS

TEACHERS' LOUNGE

School

by Joan Holub   pictures by James Dean

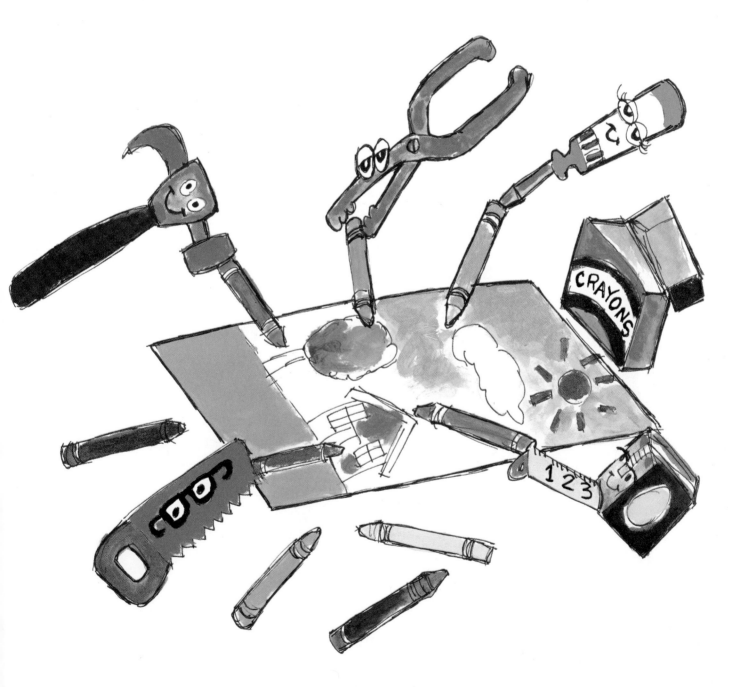

SCHOLASTIC INC.

Bonkity bonk—
Bam! Bam! Bam!

I'm a little tool, a Hammer I am.
I bam all day, and I bonk all night.
'Cause I like to bang things with all my might!

Twist and turn—
Poke! Poke! Poke!

I'm a Screwdriver, and that's no joke.
Watch me twist left. I can twist right, too.
I'll tighten or loosen any screw!

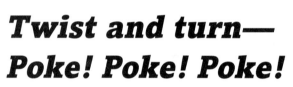

Open and close—
Pinch! Pinch! Pinch!

I'm called Pliers, and my job's a cinch.
First I open up my sharky jaws.
Then I clamp on tight like lobster claws!

Back and forth—
Bite! Bite! Bite!

I'm a little Saw with teeth. That's right!
Flash! goes my blade all shiny clean.
I'm lean. I'm mean. I'm a cutting machine!

Stretch, stretch, stretch—
1, 2, 3!

I'm a Tape Measure with numbers, see?
I measure short, and I measure long.
My inches and feet are never wrong!

We're five little tools who love to learn,
with big ideas and energy to burn.
We may be small, but our skills are cool.
Let's go build on them at our new school!

With smiles and waves, we hop on the bus.
At school, there's a classroom just for us.

Look! Cubbies with wood, cardboard, and glue.
Hey! Nails, screws, clamps, and a teacher, too!

"Welcome, tools! Come and sit inside.
I'm Ms. Drill," she says, smiling wide.

WELCOME
TO
TOOL SCHOOL!

CRAYONS

"We're going to have fun. We'll work and play.
Are you ready to make some friends today?"

We read, do puzzles, and learn some games.
We decorate tags that tell our names.

We sing fun rhymes about famous tools
and songs to remember safety rules.

Now teacher says, "Give your skills a try."
We get excited, and that's no lie.
We grab supplies from the classroom shelf.
It's time to build. *Every tool for itself!*

All five of us tools start to work alone,
each trying to make something on our own.

"I can't."

"Mine's a mess."

"Don't give up, tools. Be a can-do crew.
Let's talk this out and try something new.
Working by yourself can be fun galore.
But sometimes a job takes two or more.

Know what you need? It could save the day:
COOPERATION. Say it now, okay?"

This time, could they really build something great
if they did their best to cooperate?

We tools get busy, fired up to begin.
Working as a team, we all will win.
Mistakes are made, but we all pitch in.
To finish, you have to try, try again!

We each take turns, saying thanks and please.
Construction problems become a breeze!
We smile. We cheer. We give compliments.
Which boost our whole team's confidence!

Bam! Poke!
Pinch! Bite!
Strreeetch!

What fun!
The time zooms by.
Soon our project is . . .

The five little tools shout hip-hooray!
They'd learned cool stuff and had a great day.
Heading home, they call to their new friends,
"See you tomorrow, and we'll build again!"

COOL TOOL TIPS

Hammer:
Keep your fingers out of harm's
way when you bam a hammer.
Hold a hammer firmly so it
won't fly out of your hand.

Screwdriver:
You'll need a flat-head screwdriver like
me for screws with a single-line slot.
A Phillips screwdriver has an X-shape
tip for screws with an X-shape slot.

Saw:
I am a crosscut saw. I cut across
the grain of the wood. My special
sharp teeth help me cut when I push
and when I pull to cleanly slice
through the wood's grain.

Pliers:
Some pliers are for gripping
something round like a pipe. Others
are for twisting wires or other tasks.
Always use the right pliers for the job.

Tape Measure:
Measure twice, cut once.
Smart tools always double-check their
measurements before cutting with a saw.

Ms. Drill:
Always have a grown-up
around to help when
you use tools.

ALWAYS WORK WITH A GROWN-UP AND WEAR SAFETY GOGGLES.

AND FOR GOOD MEASURE, NEVER BAM, POKE, PINCH, OR BITE YOUR FRIENDS!